Martha Says It with Flowers

Based on a teleplay written by Peter K. Hirsch

Based on characters created by Susan Meddaugh

Houghton Mifflin Harcourt

Boston • New York

Copyright © 2010 WGBH Educational Foundation and Susan Meddaugh. "MARTHA" and all characters and underlying materials (including artwork) from the "MARTHA" books are copyright, trademarks, and registered trademarks of Susan Meddaugh and used under license. All other characters and materials are copyright and trademarks of WGBH. All rights reserved. The PBS KIDS logo is a registered mark of PBS and is used with permission.

For information about permission to reproduce selections from this book, write to Permissions, Houghton Mifflin Harcourt Publishing Company, 215 Park Avenue South, New York, New York 10003.

Green Light Readers and its logo are trademarks of Houghton Mifflin Harcourt Publishing Company.

Library of Congress Cataloging-in-Publication Data is on file.
ISBN 978-0-547-37159-7
Design by Stephanie Cooper and Rachel Newborn
www.hmhbooks.com | www.marthathetalkingdog.com
Manufactured in China | LEO 10 9 8 7 6 5 4 3 2
4500271566

Martha was always a thoughtful dog. She was eager to please with a kind word or a helpful suggestion.

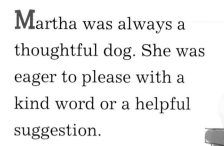

> Mom said that fruitcake you made wasn't fit for a dog, but I thought it was delicious!

> I'd like to add to our order. After all, what's a plain cheese pizza without bacon, pepperoni, and hamburger?

But as much as she wanted to help, some people were so hard to please, like Helen's grandmother Lucille.

One day, as Grandma Lucille was leaving Martha's house, she
suddenly remembered something.

"Oh dear, I left my hat inside," she said.

"I'll get it!" said Martha.

She quickly returned with the hat in her mouth. But now it
was crumpled and covered with bite marks and drool.

"You've ruined my hat!" cried Grandma Lucille.

I only wanted to be helpful, thought Martha. *I guess I'll have to try harder.*

"If you want Grandma to forgive you for ruining her hat, maybe you could do something nice for her on her birthday," suggested Helen.

Great idea!

The next day Martha walked into Helen's room with a muddy piece of paper in her mouth.

"I told the next-door neighbor what to write," Martha said.

Helen took the card and opened it.

"Happy one hundredth birthday," she read.

"It was kind of you to make a card, but Grandma Lucille isn't turning one hundred," Helen told Martha.

"I always have trouble figuring out age in human years," said Martha.

"Maybe you should *get* her something instead. The Wagging Tail Gift Shop might give you an idea," Helen suggested.

"Helen was right," said Martha.

She found the perfect present in an alley right next to the Wagging Tail Gift Shop.

"Grandma Lucille is going to love this!"

She saw Grandpa Bernie inside the store, and went in to show him her present.

"Martha! This is a half-eaten rotten apple!" Grandpa Bernie exclaimed.

I don't think Grandma Lucille will like it.

"Really?" said Martha. "Did you notice the worm? I'd love to get this as a gift."

But Grandpa Bernie said, "You might want to get her something that a person would like."

Pleasing Grandma Lucille is not easy, thought Martha.

Martha left the Wagging Tail Gift Shop feeling very discouraged. But when she passed the butcher shop, she had an inspiration.

Dogs like it and people like it, she thought.

Skits liked it too.

"Woof!" he said.

"No," Martha told him. "This is not for us. This is for Grandma Lucille."

Bacon, the perfect present!

But when Martha brought home the bacon, Mariela said, "Oh, dear. Grandma Lucille doesn't eat bacon. We'll just save this for our breakfast tomorrow."

Skits licked his chops, but Martha was too worried to even drool.

Now she had to find another present, and Grandma Lucille's birthday was coming soon.

Uh-oh. Wrong again.

I can't seem to do anything right for Grandma Lucille, thought Martha. *My gifts were all mistakes. I insulted her fruitcake. I ruined her favorite hat with the fake flowers.*

Then Martha had another inspired idea.

"Flowers," she said. "That's the perfect present!"

She got a basket and trotted off to the park with Skits.

Real flowers are always better than fake flowers!

"I know Grandma Lucille likes flowers," Martha told Skits. "She had some on her hat."

She gathered a bunch to take home.

Martha hid the flowers behind the chair in the living room for safekeeping.

The days passed quickly. Soon it was time for Grandma Lucille's birthday party!

Martha walked behind the chair to get the flowers, but . . .

Oh, no—what happened to Grandma Lucille's flowers?

They were all dry and crumbly.

"Are you ready to go to the birthday party, Martha?" Helen asked.
"Not quite," said Martha. "You go ahead and I'll meet you there."

I hope!

Martha had to get some new flowers, and fast!

It didn't take long to find a nice patch of flowers. With her basket full, Martha climbed aboard a bus that would take her close to Grandma Lucille's house.

"Those are lovely flowers," the man sitting next to Martha said.

"Thank you! They're for Grandma Lucille's birthday," said Martha. "Would you like to have one, sir?"

"How kind of you!" he said. "I'll just take this little blue one, and maybe a yellow . . ."

A little girl wanted a flower too, and Martha gave her one. It made the girl happy. Then Martha gave some more flowers to the other people on the bus.

"Everyone loved getting flowers. I am such a thoughtful dog," Martha said as she climbed off the bus.

Martha looked into her basket.
Oh, no! *Only a few flowers left,* she thought. *But they're still pretty.*
She started walking to Grandma Lucille's.

She hadn't gone far when she saw something so wonderful, she dropped her basket of flowers. It was a man dressed like a hamburger, and he was giving out free samples.

I'll just eat this hamburger and then be on my way,
Martha thought.

But it was so hard to stop after only one.

"Time to go," said Martha, and she looked for her basket.

Oh, no!

Birds were carrying away the flowers.

"Stop!" yelled Martha. "It's not nice to take my flowers."

Martha looked into the basket. There was only one flower left. Then it started to rain.

When Martha got to Grandma Lucille's, she was wet and tired, but she still had one beautiful flower. Then just as the door was opened, the wind blew the petals away from her last flower.

"Happy birthday, Grandma Lucille," said Martha. "I had a whole basket of fresh flowers for you and now they're all gone, and I know how much you like flowers because of your hat, and, oh, I tried so hard . . ."

I'm sorry.

Martha was surprised when Grandma Lucille said, "Well, I'm very glad that you got rid of them. I'm allergic to *real* flowers. They make me sneeze."

A soggy Martha came inside.

"You're just trying to make me feel better," Martha said.

"No," Grandma Lucille told her. "I really mean it. But here's something I know will make you feel better."

She brought a plate from the table, and Martha discovered that she still had room for cake.

After eating her cake, Martha jumped up on the couch to take a nap.
"Oh, no," said Grandpa Bernie. "She's still wet."
But Grandma Lucille said, "That's all right. Not every family has such a considerate dog."